Snap books™

10 Things You Need to Know About

Looking Great

by Jen Jones

Capstone
press®

Mankato, Minnesota

Snap Books are published by Capstone Press,
151 Good Counsel Drive, P.O. Box 669, Mankato, Minnesota 56002.
www.capstonepress.com

Library of Congress Cataloging-in-Publication Data
Jones, Jen.
    Looking great / by Jen Jones.
    p. cm. — (Snap books. 10 things you need to know about)
    Summary: "Provides helpful information on personal care for girls, including tips on skin care, makeup,
nutrition, and fashion" — Provided by publisher.
    Includes bibliographical references and index.
    ISBN-13: 978-1-4296-1344-6 (hardcover)
    ISBN-10: 1-4296-1344-0 (hardcover)
    1. Teenage girls — Life skills guides. 2. Teenage girls — Health and hygiene. 3. Girls — Life skills guides.
4. Girls — Health and hygiene. 5. Beauty, Personal. 6. Grooming for girls. I. Title. II. Series.
HQ798.J66 2008
646.7'046 — dc22
                                          2007028291

Editors: Kathryn Clay and Christine Peterson
Designer: Juliette Peters
Photo Researcher: Jo Miller
Photo Stylist: Kelly Garvin

Photo Credits:
All photos by Capstone Press/Karon Dubke, except Michele Torma Lee, 32

1 2 3 4 5 6 13 12 11 10 09 08

Table of Contents

Introduction

Ever heard the saying, "Beauty is in the eye of the beholder?" It means that each person sees beauty differently. Some people love the look of red roses, while others prefer yellow daisies. When it comes to personal appearance, the same rule applies. Some girls love loud colors for hair and makeup, while others go for a softer, more natural look. Short, tall, curly, straight — no single look sets the beauty standard.

In this book, you'll discover how to achieve your personal beauty best. You'll learn insider secrets on everything from zapping zits to taming your tresses. Most importantly, you'll learn how to showcase your strengths rather than fret about your flaws. Get ready to glow from head to toe.

Beauty isn't "one size fits all"

Whether you're stick-thin or curvy-cute, it's natural to feel self-conscious about your body type. After all, society often makes girls feel like they have to fit a certain mold. But beauty comes in all shapes and sizes. Looking great is all about feeling great. If you can accept the skin you're in, you'll project a confidence that is simply irresistible.

Dress for Success

Want to flaunt what you've got? Learn which clothes flatter your body type.

❀ Hourglass figures shine in outfits that are form fitting yet not skintight. V-neck tops and wrap dresses are smart choices.

❀ Full-figures look great in dark colors and vertical stripes — both have a snazzy slimming effect. Other can't-miss clothes include pants without pockets and shirtdresses.

❀ Straight figures can add shape with funky belts, A-line skirts, or dresses. Halter tops and low-rise jeans also create the illusion of curves.

2 Treat your locks with love

Feel like every day is a bad hair day? Follow these tips, and you're sure to be voted your school's "best-tressed."

❁ Shampoo only as often as needed. Believe it or not, hair doesn't have to be washed every day. Doing so can dry hair out. When you do shampoo, rinse thoroughly. Afterward, remember to finish up with a good conditioner.

❁ Cut loose! Short styles should be cut every month for upkeep. Long locks can go six to eight weeks between salon trips. Following this time line will help keep split ends away.

❁ Turn down the heat. Do you use a flat iron or blow-dryer? Save your strands by using a heat protection styling product. To reduce frizz, point your blow-dryer down when drying your hair.

Brushing Basics

When your mother was a teen, her beauty ritual may have included brushing her hair 100 times a day. But times have changed. Today's stylists know that over-brushing your hair leads to damage. Hair only needs a gentle brushing to get rid of troublesome tangles.

3 A smile will take you the extra mile

Smiles not only light up the room, they also light up your face. Flashing those pearly whites is an easy shortcut to an A+ appearance. If you have braces or discolored teeth, you might be a little shy about sharing your smile. Try these tips for a glowing grin:

❀ Say good-bye to soda and coffee. These drinks can stain teeth and chip away at enamel. If you can't resist these beverages, then drink them with a straw to protect your teeth.

❀ Brighten up. Lots of whitening products are on today's market — from mouthwashes to gels to toothpastes. If you'd rather go with a homemade solution, baking soda does the trick. Just dip your toothbrush in the dry powder and brush as usual.

❀ Talk about heavy metal. If you have braces, use soft lip gloss or matte colors instead of shiny lipsticks. This will attract attention away from your braces and give you something to smile about.

4 Work it, baby, work it!

Want to achieve a radiant glow? Exercise is the secret. Staying active gets your blood flowing and gives your skin a healthy look. Plus when you sweat, your body releases toxins, leaving you pleasantly pimple-free.

Even better, exercise helps you stay in shape. From yoga to kickboxing to swimming, tons of activities exist for all interests and fitness levels. It's not about being the thinnest girl on the block. Looking great is all about becoming the healthiest version of you.

Super Snacks

These fab energy-boosting foods get you ready for exercise. They're also secret beauty weapons.

❀ Almonds keep your skin smooth and clear, thanks to a high amount of vitamin E. Peaches and blueberries are other great sources of vitamin E.

❀ Rev up with high-fiber foods like apples and celery, which also help remove plaque from teeth.

❀ Say "cheese!" Calcium-rich cheese will strengthen your nails and bones.

5
For a "polished" look, focus on your nails

Want to pamper yourself like a princess? Treat yourself to a manicure and pedicure. Visiting the salon is fun, but you can also do these treatments in the comfort of your own home. Follow these steps for amazing do-it-yourself nails.

TRUSTY TOOLS

cotton balls	cuticle stick
nail polish remover	moisturizing lotion
nail file	base coat polish
mild soap	nail polish
honey	top coat polish
cuticle cream	

1. Remove old nail polish using cotton balls and nail polish remover.

2. Use a nail file to achieve your desired shape. Some girls like rounded nails, while others prefer a squared-off look. For pedis, file nails straight across to avoid pesky hangnails.

3. For manis, soak fingernails in soapy water for a few minutes. For pedis, soak feet in warm water for up to 10 minutes. Add a little honey for super-sweet results.

4. After soaking, apply cuticle cream. Use a cuticle stick to push back cuticles.

5. Wash your hands or feet, and then soothe the skin by rubbing in moisturizing lotion.

6. Paint a base coat onto the nails. Let dry for one minute. This will help your manicure last longer.

7. Apply two coats of your favorite polish. Feel free to go crazy with color, or class it up with clear polish.

8. After the polish dries, seal the deal with a clear top coat. You're now the proud owner of great looking nails.

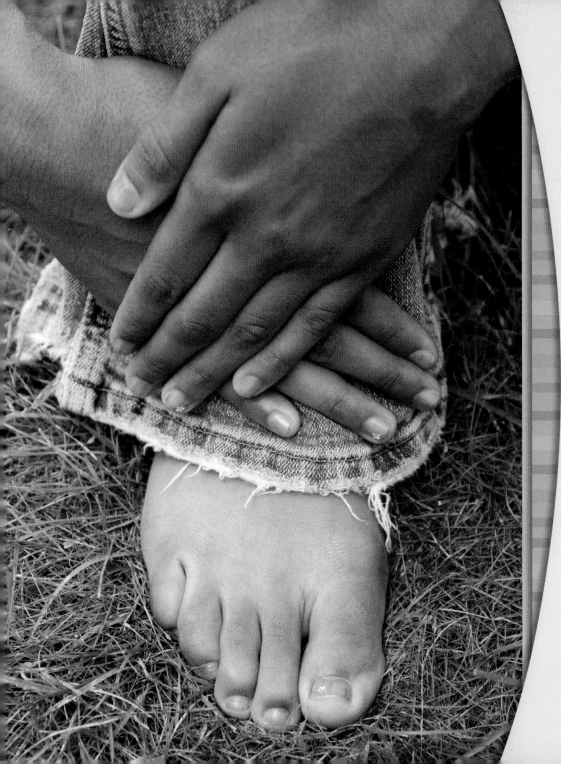

Finger Tip

Do your nails chip easily or look unhealthy? Strengthen your nails by soaking them in extra-virgin olive oil for 15 minutes each day.

6 Say bye-bye to blemishes

Putting your best face forward can be difficult when you're battling an acne breakout. Acne naturally comes with the teen territory, but clear skin can be yours with a simple daily routine.

❁ Follow the "2 x 2" rule. Wash your face two times, twice a day. The first wash cleans off makeup. The second wash rids your skin of dirt and buildup. Got oily skin? Use an oil-free cleansing gel.

❁ Stop the popping. Though it might be tempting to pop your pimple, doing so can make the zit look even worse. (It may even leave a scar!) Be patient, and your pimples will go away naturally.

❁ Kiss dry skin good-bye. Using a good moisturizer will keep your skin hydrated. Some moisturizers even include sunscreen or can act as foundation. Talk about multi-talented!

To the Rescue

For serious acne cases, do-it-yourself care might not do the trick. Luckily, a good dermatologist can save the day. Talk to your parents about seeing a dermatologist who can suggest treatments that may work for you.

Think of makeup as icing on a cake. You don't need a lot to make a big difference. Tons of makeup products are on the shelf. But just a few essentials can work wonders.

❀ Makeup artists suggest going against your eye color. Blue shades bring out brown eyes, while browns and beiges complement blue eyes. For green eyes, soft purples and pinks do the trick.

❀ Young girls don't need heavy, all-over foundation. Instead, buy a simple stick foundation to dot over zits.

❀ Blush gives your cheeks a rosy glow. Soft shades of pink, peach, or bronze add color without going overboard. Not sure where to apply it? Smile to find the "apple," or round part, of your cheek.

❀ When you're crunched for time, lip gloss and mascara are all you need to go glam. Pale or clear lip gloss adds serious shine, while black mascara really makes your eyes stand out.

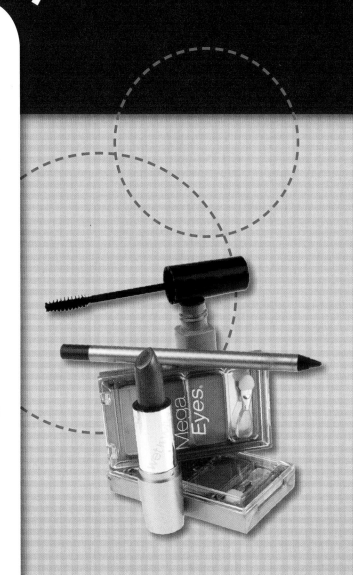

8 Put your best face forward

Want another secret shortcut to looking great? It's simple: create "wow" brows. You'll be surprised how a few well-placed plucks can change your appearance. Let's face the facts. Sometimes our eyebrows just won't behave. Luckily, plucking and waxing can whip them into shape. Though waxing is best left to salon pros, you can do a few taming tricks on your own.

❀ Eyebrow powder can be your new best friend for shaping. For color, go one shade darker for light hair and one shade lighter for dark hair. Comb brows with an eyebrow brush, then use the brush to apply the powder. Start at the inner corner, moving outward with light strokes. Try to color just the hair, not the skin.

❀ Clear mascara provides another quick brow fix. The mascara defines brows and holds them in place.

Caution!

Plan to pluck your own brows? Proceed with care! Going overboard could leave you with pencil-thin brows. Instead of going crazy plucking, use a small nail scissors to trim stray hairs.

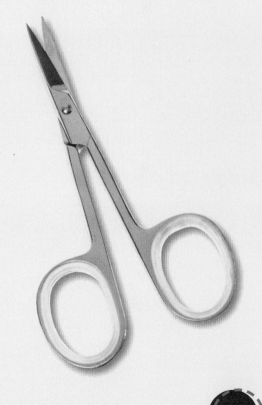

9 Spa treatments don't have to cost a fortune

Just like at-home manicures and pedicures, there are oodles of do-it-yourself spa treatments. Check out these popular at-home spa recipes.

HONEY OATMEAL FACIAL

What You Need: ½ cup oatmeal, 2 tablespoons honey, 1 teaspoon lemon juice, ¼ cup plain yogurt

How You Do It: Start by processing the oatmeal in a blender. In a small bowl, stir the honey, lemon juice, and yogurt together. Add the oatmeal. Mix it all together until it becomes a paste. Smooth it over your face and neck. Leave the paste on for 15 minutes, and then rinse off with warm water.

STRAWBERRY HAND AND FOOT SCRUB

What You Need: 10 strawberries, 2 tablespoons olive oil, 1 teaspoon kosher salt or sea salt, 2 tablespoons chopped almonds

How You Do It: Mix all the ingredients together to form a paste. Massage the paste into your hands or feet. Rinse off, pat dry, and say good-bye to dead skin cells.

10 Great from the inside out

Taking good care of yourself can sometimes take a backseat. But it's important to spend time nourishing what's on the inside. Here's how:

❀ Mom was right when she told you to take your vitamins. Vitamin B keeps your skin, nails, and hair healthy. Vitamin C takes care of your teeth and gums. The list of vitamin benefits goes on and on.

❀ Beauty sleep isn't just a funny saying. Sleep is often sacrificed for social or school duties. Yet lack of rest can lead to puffy eyes, dark circles under your eyes, and a lack of energy. Try to get at least 8 ½ hours of sleep each night — your body will thank you.

❀ Looking great starts within. If you believe that you are attractive, others will be attracted to you. Life is too short to worry about things we can't change. Take time to appreciate your appearance each morning. Confidence is truly beautiful.

Lovely Locks

Want to know the secret for gorgeous hair? It's as easy as raiding the kitchen pantry. Rinsing with apple cider vinegar adds some serious shine, while olive oil can repair damaged hair.

H2O Glow

There's plenty of water to go around. In fact, water covers 70 percent of the earth's surface. Do yourself a favor by drinking at least seven glasses each day. Water helps you maintain a healthy weight, clear your skin, and stay hydrated.

Color Your World

Want a new look that's sure to get noticed? Hair color might be just what the beauty doctor ordered. It may be tempting to go from brunette to platinum blonde. But most stylists recommend staying within two shades of your natural locks. If you don't want to change your all-over color, try transforming your tresses with highlights or bold streaks.

It's Tea Time!

Products made from tea trees cure all kinds of beauty problems, including acne. With a cotton swab, apply a dab of tea tree oil directly to your zit. After several daily applications, your zit will be going . . . going . . . gone!

Quiz

What Type of Beauty Queen Are You?

Your morning beauty ritual:
- A What morning beauty ritual?
- B Involves a quick hair and makeup fix
- C Lasts for hours

You're stranded on a desert island. What's your must-have beauty item?
- A A bar of soap
- B Hairbrush
- C Mascara

Which celeb shares your sense of style?
- A Amanda Bynes
- B Hilary Duff
- C Christina Aguilera

Which store would you choose for a $500 shopping spree?
- A Target
- B Wet Seal
- C Sephora

What's your biggest beauty issue?
- A Applying makeup the right way
- B Finding different ways to change up my look
- C So many products, so little time

Woo-hoo! A day at the spa! What treatment do you choose?
- A Massage
- B Facial
- C Body scrub

What color are you wearing on your nails right now?
- A Clear polish
- B French manicure
- C Glam red

What's your go-to method for whiter teeth?
- A Good ol' toothpaste
- B Whitening strips
- C Laser whitening

How do you go about getting a tan?

(A) Why bother?

(B) Add a tiny dash of bronzer

(●) With a lifetime supply of self-tanner

How often do you change your hairstyle?

(A) If it isn't broke, why fix it?

(B) My flat iron and curling iron get their fair share of exercise.

(●) At each monthly salon appointment, of course!

If you could have a bedroom makeover, what would you add?

(A) A private bathroom

(B) A walk-in closet

(●) A massive vanity

What's your take on waxing?

(A) The "ouch" factor is way too high

(B) Maybe for eyebrows, but that's it

(●) I'm all about it — shaving is so yesterday!

How do you keep your skin gorgeous?

(A) Eating right

(B) Making sure to remove makeup every night

(●) Eye cream, moisturizer, toner . . . the list goes on and on

What's your fave must-read magazine?

(A) *Girls' Life*

(B) *CosmoGIRL!*

(●) *Lucky*

Name your lip product of choice:

(A) Lip balm

(B) Lip gloss

(●) Lipstick

When scoring your answers, (A) equals 5 points, (B) equals 3 points, and (●) equals 1 point. Total them up and find out your appearance approach!

1–25 = Hey there, glamour girl! No doubt you make a fab beauty junkie. But don't forget to also nurture what's under the surface.

26–50 = You're no beauty school dropout. You've got a great outlook on looking great.

51–75 = For you, less is more. Don't be afraid to play up your natural beauty sometimes.

29

Glossary

cuticle (KYOO-tuh-kuhl) — the tough layer of dead skin around the edges of your nails

dermatologist (dur-muh-TOL-uh-jist) — a doctor who specializes in treating skin disorders

enamel (ih-NA-muhl) — a hard, white substance found on teeth

hydrate (HYE-drayt) — to achieve a healthy balance of fluids in the body

matte (MAT) — not shiny

pamper (PAM-pur) — to take good care of yourself or others

ritual (RICH-oo-uhl) — a set of actions that is always performed the same way

toxin (TOK-sin) — a substance produced by a living thing that can often be poisonous

Read More

Haberman, Lia. *About Face: Beauty Tricks & Tips.* Makeover Fun 101. New York: Scholastic, 2005.

Kauchak, Therese. *The Real Beauty: 101 Ways to Feel Great About You.* Middleton, Wis.: Pleasant Company, 2004.

Traig, Jennifer. *Makeup: Things to Make and Do.* Crafty Girl. San Francisco: Chronicle Books, 2003.

Internet Sites

FactHound offers a safe, fun way to find Internet sites related to this book. All of the sites on FactHound have been researched by our staff.

Here's how:
1. Visit *www.facthound.com*
2. Choose your grade level.
3. Type in this book ID **1429613440** for age-appropriate sites. You may also browse subjects by clicking on letters, or by clicking on pictures and words.
4. Click on the **Fetch It** button.

FactHound will fetch the best sites for you!

About the Author

When Jen Jones isn't writing the day away at her laptop, she can be found shopping at makeup counters or treating herself to a well-deserved manicure! She is a Los Angeles-based writer who has authored more than 30 books for Capstone Press. Her stories have been published in magazines such as *American Cheerleader*, *Dance Spirit*, *Ohio Today*, and *Pilates Style*. She has also written for *E! Online* and *PBS Kids*, and has been a Web site producer for major talk shows such as *The Jenny Jones Show*, *The Sharon Osbourne Show*, and *The Larry Elder Show*.

Index